Laura Owen and Korky Paul

Winnie
to the Rescue!

OXFORD
UNIVERSITY PRESS

For my kids, Zoë and Oska – K.P.
In loving memory of Elsie Goodhart – xx

This World Book Day book first published in Great Britain
by Oxford University Press / Simon and Schuster Ltd, 2009
'Itchy Witchy' first published in *Winnie Says Cheese* 2009
and 'Winnie's Book Day' first published in *Whizz-Bang Winnie* 2008 by:

OXFORD
UNIVERSITY PRESS

Great Clarendon Street, Oxford OX2 6DP

Oxford University Press is a department of the University of Oxford.
It furthers the University's objective of excellence in research, scholarship,
and education by publishing worldwide in

Oxford   New York

Auckland   Cape Town   Dar es Salaam   Hong Kong   Karachi
Kuala Lumpur   Madrid   Melbourne   Mexico City   Nairobi
New Delhi   Shanghai   Taipei   Toronto

With offices in
Argentina   Austria   Brazil   Chile   Czech Republic   France   Greece
Guatemala   Hungary   Italy   Japan   Poland   Portugal   Singapore
South Korea   Switzerland   Thailand   Turkey   Ukraine   Vietnam

Oxford is a registered trade mark of Oxford University Press
in the UK and in certain other countries

Text © Oxford University Press 2008, 2009
Illustrations © Korky Paul 2008, 2009
The characters in this work are the original creation of Valerie Thomas
who retains copyright in the characters

British Library Cataloguing in Publication Data:
Data available

ISBN: 978-0-95594466-6 (paperback)

2 4 6 8 10 9 7 5 3 1

Printed by CPI Cox & Wyman, Reading, Berkshire RG1 8EX

Paper used in the production of this book is a natural, recyclable product made
from wood grown in sustainable forests. The manufacturing process conforms
to the environmental regulations of the country of origin.

This book has been specially published for World Book Day 2009.
World Book Day is a worldwide celebration of books and reading, and was marked
in over 30 countries around the globe last year. For further information please see
www.worldbookday.com

World Book Day in the UK and Ireland is made possible by generous sponsorship from
National Book Tokens, participating publishers, authors and booksellers. Booksellers who
accept the £1 World Book Day Token kindly agree to bear the full cost of redeeming it.

contents

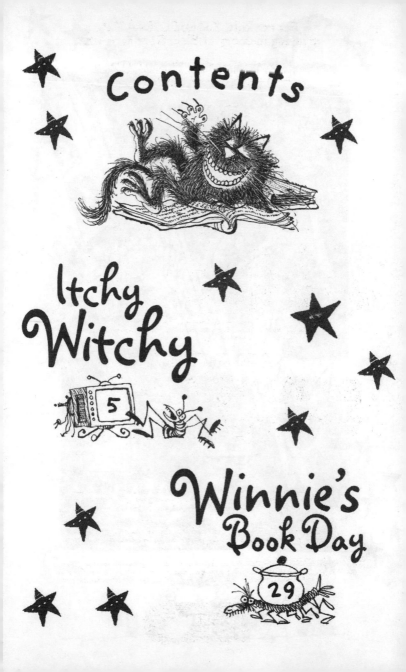

Itchy Witchy

Winnie held the telling-moan away from her ear and winced at big sister Wanda's voice.

'Are you listening, Winnie?' screeched Wanda. 'The witches' cat show is tomorrow. I'm putting Wayne in for it, of course. He won it last year, you know. I've just had his teeth whitened. And highlights put in his fur.'

Wayne was Wanda's snooty sleek-as-a-panther cat.

'Have you still got that scraggy old catty thing of yours?' asked Wanda. 'What was he called?'

'He's called Wilbur,' said Winnie. 'And he's lovely.'

'Well, we'll all see just how lovely he is at the show, won't we! He hee!' laughed Wanda.

6

'No,' said Winnie. 'I wasn't going to—'

'He hee! He hee!' cackled Wanda. 'I knew it! I said to Wayne, I said, "I bet Winnie won't dare to put that Wilbur in for the show because she knows very well he'll come bottom of the whole thing!" He heee! I just knew it!'

Winnie glared at the telling-moan. 'Well, you knew wrong, Wanda the Witch!' she said. 'The only bottom thing at the show will be your Wayne winning the competition for the cat who has the witch with the biggest bottom—YOURS! Wilbur *will* be in the show, and he might just win it! So there!'

Winnie slammed down the telling-moan.
Then she chewed a nail. 'Oh, banana
bandages!' she said to herself. 'Winnie
the Witch, whatever have you gone and
done now?'

Winnie looked at Wilbur lying happily in the sun. There was a spider's web stuck between Wilbur's ears. There was a bald patch on his back where he'd rolled around on hot tar and it had pulled some of his fur off. There was some pond slime hanging from his tail. And flies were hovering over him in a way that suggested that he might not be smelling very fresh at the moment.

Winnie found a pair of shark-fin scissors, some carpet shampoo, a big bottle of skunk scent, a brush, a comb, some slug-slime hair gel, some gizzard glue and a ball of black wool, and she took them all outside.

'Oh, Wilbur!' she called.

Wilbur opened one eye.

'Come to Winnie, Wilbur!' called Winnie.

Wilbur's ears went flat onto his head. Up he leapt, and he was about to run when—

'**Abracadabra!**' went Winnie, and instantly poor Wilbur was frozen still. 'I'm sorry about this, Wilbur, but I've got to make you beautiful,' said Winnie.

Winnie got to work, washing . . . and combing . . . and sticking wool over bald bits. And then she saw a little something **hop-hop-HOP** in Wilbur's fur.

13

'Oh, heck, Wilbur, you've got fleas!'
said Winnie. She caught the flea mid-hop
and popped it into her mouth. 'Mmm,'
she said. 'Quite tasty in a tickle-your-
taste-buds kind of way, but I don't think
they give you a prize at the show if you've
got fleas. Come on, Wilbur. We're off to
the vet's to get you some flea treatment,'
said Winnie.

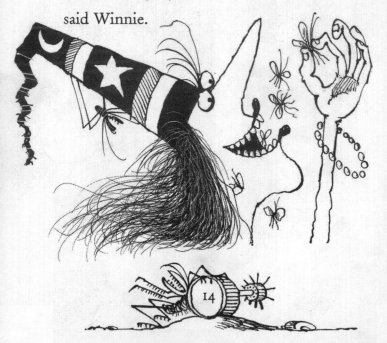

14

Winnie un-froze Wilbur once he was inside the carrying box. It's horrible being in a box. There's nowhere to hide. Wilbur felt the jolting and swaying as Winnie got off her broomstick and carried the box into the surgery. Then he smelt that vetty smell.

15

'Meeeeoooowww!' he wailed miserably.

'My goodness,' said the vet. 'When did this animal last see a vet?'

'Oh, ages ago,' said Winnie. 'He hates vets.'

'Mrrrow!' went Wilbur, then he showed just how much he hated vets by scrabbling up this one and sitting on his head. He took off the vet's toupee when Winnie lifted him down.

'Is that an animal that went up and died there?' asked Winnie.

16

The vet squirted stuff on to Wilbur to get rid of the fleas. The fleas march-hopped—cough, sneeze!—down off Wilbur and on to Winnie and the vet. *Itch-itch, scratch.*

'Now,' said the vet. *Itch, scratch.* 'This cat needs injections for cat flu and cat cold and cat sore-throat and cat ingrowing toenails and cat tennis elbow.'

'Are you sure?' said Winnie. 'How much will that lot cost?'

'Let me see,' said the vet, and he began poking numbers into his calculator. **Itch, scratch.** Winnie saw a number getting longer and longer.

'Quick, Wilbur!' she whispered. 'Let's go!'

Wilbur did look very smart at the show, even if he didn't look happy. Winnie felt worried and **itch-itch** scratchy.

But Wanda and Wayne were smug-as-a-bug happy. Wayne lounged in a suave and sophisticated smiley way.

20

'What do you think of my Wayne, then, Winnie? Just feel how silky his fur is. Go on, Win, have a feel!' said Wanda.

So Winnie reached out a hand to feel how soft Wayne was. And as she touched him . . . this hopped . . . and that hopped . . . and those hopped . . . off Winnie and on to Wayne. **Itch-itch, scratch. Itch-itch-itch, scritchety-scratch.**

'Oo, here comes the judge!' said Wanda.

'Just watch what he says about Wayne and Wilbur, he hee!' *Itch-scratch,* went Wayne. 'Don't do that, Wayne darling,' said Wanda. 'Be nice for the judge.'

The judge poked at Wilbur first.

'Mrrrow!' went Wilbur. He'd had enough of being poked for one day.

The judge lifted Wilbur's tail.

'Hisss!' Scratch! went Wilbur.

'Disqualified!' said the judge.

'He heee!' said Wanda.

The judge poked at Wayne.

'Purrrr!' went Wayne.

The judge lifted Wayne's tail.

'Purrr!' Smarm! went Wayne.

'Very nice indeed,' said the judge.

But just then—*itch*, went Wayne. *Itch-itch, scratch-scratch.* And then the judge felt an itch and began to scratch.

'Uh!' he shouted, snatching his hands away from Wayne. 'This cat has got FLEAS!'

He was about to disqualify Wayne, but there was no need to because everybody was disqualifying themselves, running and shoving to get away from the fleas and the show.

'What a lot of fuss over a few fleas!' said Winnie, happily scratching herself. 'Call themselves witches! Huh! Come on, let's go home, Wilbur.'

Back home Wilbur rolled in the grass to get himself back to himself.

'Here's a rosette for you!' said Winnie, and she fixed a dried tarantula to his ear. 'It's for being the best cat for me!'

'Purrr!' said Wilbur proudly.

They sat and ate squashed-flea biscuits. And all the fleas that had fled to Winnie's head, hopped back on to Wilbur because Wilbur tasted nicer, if you were a flea.

And so all the fleas were back home, too. Except for one adventurous flea who had hopped on to Wayne and then on to Wanda because he liked the taste of her hair spray. So Wanda was going **itch-itch, scritchety-scratch.**

Hee heee!

27

Winnie's Book Day

'I'm bored!' said Winnie. 'I'm as bored as a snail is bored with the view inside its shell. I'm as bored as my toes are with the smell inside my socks. I'm as bored as . . .'

'Mrrow!' said Wilbur, and he put his paws over his ears.

'Am I being boring, Wilbur?' said Winnie.

'Mrrow!' said Wilbur crossly.

'What do people do to stop being bored?

29

Let's go down to the village and look in the library,' said Winnie.

The library was full of bookshelves, and full of people reading books.

'Look at them!' whispered Winnie. One person was laughing. Another looked frightened. 'How do books do that to people?' asked Winnie. She took a book from a shelf and looked at the black words on a white page that she couldn't read.

Those marks didn't make her cry or laugh or feel anything. Winnie turned the book the other way up, but it didn't make any difference. Wilbur was lying on the carpet with a book open in front of him and he was cat-laughing.

'Mrow-ha-ha!'

'I want to know what's funny!' said Winnie. 'I'm blooming well going back to that school!'

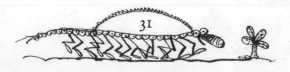

Winnie was in luck.

'Look at that, Wilbur! There's a whole flock of witches going to school today! And girls with plaits and stripy stockings and bears with suitcases and wizards with zigzags on their foreheads and . . . oh . . . almost everything except little ordinaries. They're as odd as a bag of ugly bug pick-n-mix. Come on, Wilbur, we'll fit in with the others today!'

'Who are you?' asked one small witch
in stripy tights.

'I'm Winnie the Witch,' said Winnie.

'So am I!' said the small one.

'Eh?' Winnie stood still and puzzled.

'How does that work, then?'

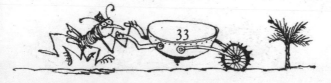

33

But Wilbur caught her cardigan in a claw and hurried her into the classroom.

The teacher, in a red cloak with a hood, was taking the register.

'Captain Teachum?'

'Here.'

'Professor Puffendorf?'

'Here.'

'Winnie the Witch?'

'Here,' said the little girl who had talked to Winnie earlier.

'Here,' said Winnie.

'Who are you?' asked the teacher, glaring at Winnie. 'And what is that cat doing in my classroom? We don't allow witches in school!'

'But—!' began Winnie, looking around at lots of witches. But the teacher was pointing at the door.

'Out!' said the teacher. So Winnie and Wilbur went out of the classroom . . .

Oooff! and walked straight into Mrs Parmar, the school secretary. She was looking flustered.

'Oh, Winnie, I'm desperate!' said Mrs Parmar. 'Today is our Book Day and the dog ate all the storyteller's books, so he's not coming, and I've got children waiting for stories and nobody to tell them unless . . . oh, Winnie, could you do it? Pleeeeease?'

A smile like the crack in a boiled egg grew across Winnie's face. 'Yes!' she said.

So Mrs Parmar led Winnie and Wilbur
into the school library. Some children
were sitting on the carpet, looking up
at Winnie like vulture chicks in a nest
waiting to be fed.

'Now, children,' said Mrs Parmar.
'Winnie here is going to read to you.'

'Read?' said Winnie. 'I—' But Mrs
Parmar had already gone. 'Um,' said
Winnie. She took a book from the shelf.
'Look,' she said. 'A picture of a lion!'

'Read the story!' shouted the little extraordinaries.

'I can't!' said Winnie.

Gasp! went all the little extraordinaries.

'But,' said Winnie. 'I can make stories come out of books another way.' Winnie waved her wand. *'Abracadabra!'*

Instantly there was a great big, growly, toothy, prowly lion right inside the room! It was licking its lips and sniffing children and opening its big pink mouth wide to swallow a—

'Abracadabra!' shouted Winnie, and instantly the lion was gone. 'Phew!' said Winnie, feeling as weak as a worm. 'Er . . . wasn't that fun?'

'No!' said the little extraordinaries.

'Oh. I'll do you a better one,' said Winnie. She picked up a book with a picture of a rocket on the cover. 'Who'd like to go into space?'

'Me, me, me, me, me, me, me, me!!!'

shouted all the little extraordinaries.

Abracadabra! went Winnie.

And, instantly, there was a rocket in the room. The rocket was so big that it stuck right through the school ceiling and you could see the sky above it. Wind blustered in through the hole, making wings flutter and witchy hair whirl.

'Wow!' said the little extraordinaries, gazing up at the huge rocket.

And out of the rocket stepped a big robot spaceman.

Gasp! went the little extraordinaries.

'Fly with me to Mars,' commanded the robot. 'Together, we will fight the dreaded Xargottlenaughts!'

'Ooo, yes, let's all go to Mars!' said Winnie. 'Put on your spacesuits, everyone! Get on board.'

Winnie was hopping on one leg, trying to pull on her spacesuit. She didn't notice Wilbur sneaking out of the door. But suddenly the door burst wide open.

'WHAT ON EARTH IS GOING ON?' boomed Mrs Parmar.

'Oh!' giggled Winnie. 'It almost wasn't "what on earth", Mrs Parmar. It was almost "what on Mars"!'

Mrs Parmar inflated like a balloon. She pointed at the robot.

'You! Out! Cover your ears, children!'

They all crouched and covered their ears as the robot shut himself into his rocket and fired the engines.

ROAR!

WHOOOOOSH!

44

Up shot the rocket, leaving a great hole in the library ceiling.

'Um, that's the end of the story. *The end*,' said Winnie. So the hole closed and everything went back to normal in the library.

Mrs Parmar told the children, 'Out you

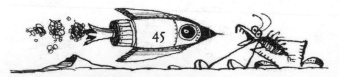

go and play.' Then she pointed at Winnie.
'You're fired!'

So Winnie and Wilbur went sadly out
to the bike shed to collect the broom.
They were just getting on board when
there was a shout from the playground.

'Help!'

A gust of wind had caught the wings
and capes of all the fairy and superhero
little extraordinaries, and they were rising
up into the sky and away from school!

'Help! Help!' they cried.

'I'm coming!' shouted Winnie.
'Hold tight, Wilbur!'

Up into the sky rose Winnie and
Wilbur on their broom. 'Grab hold
of Wilbur's paw!' Winnie told a fairy.
'Hold onto his tail!' she told a superhero.

And very soon Winnie had brought
them all safely back down to land.

'You saved the children, Winnie!'
said Mrs Parmar. 'You must come into
assembly so that the head teacher can
thank you properly.'

In assembly little Winnie the Witch
won the fancy dress prize. Big Winnie
the Witch won a medal for being a hero.

'You know what, Wilbur?' said Winnie as they walked happily home. 'There are more kinds of magic than *Abracadabra* magic.'

'Mrrow?' asked Wilbur.

'I think stories are magic too,' said Winnie.

'Purrrr,' agreed Wilbur.

Winnie and Wilbur are **itching** for
you to read more of their stories!
Available in all good bookshops.

Winnie the Witch is an accident
waiting to happen! Especially if
school dinners, DIY, rare owls or
mixed-up pets are involved . . .
ISBN 978-0-19-272576-9

Winnie the Witch loves a
challenge! Tackling a tooth fairy,
playing in a band, finding fleas,
or giving herself a makeover . . .
ISBN 978-0-19-272751-0

Winnie the Witch is ready for
anything! Awful aunties, scary school
secretaries, ghosts in the post, and
shrinking to teaspoon-size . . .
ISBN 978-0-19-272577-6

Winnie the Witch can always handle
a crisis! Losing Wilbur, rescuing kids,
feeding a fussy eater, or stopping
an out-of-control broomstick . . .
ISBN 978-0-19-272752-7

And, coming soon, look out for:

ISBN 978-0-19-272841-8

ISBN 978-0-19-272842-5

Winnie and Wilbur are waiting for you
on the web, too! Visit them both at
www.winnie-the-witch.com

MATT AND DAVE

YUCK'S
ROTTEN JOKE

Illustrated by Nigel Baines

www.yuckweb.com

There was a boy so disgusting they called him Yuck

This World Book Day book first published in Great Britain
by Oxford University Press/Simon and Schuster UK Ltd, 2009

'Yuck's Rotten Joke' originally published in *Yuck's Pet Worm*, 2007
by Simon & Schuster UK Ltd/ A CBS COMPANY/
1st floor, 222 Grays Inn Road, London WC1X 8HB

1 3 5 7 9 10 8 6 4 2

A CIP catalogue record for this book is available from the British Library

ISBN: 978-0-9559446-6-6

Printed and bound in Great Britain by
CPI Cox and Wyman, Reading, Berkshire RG1 8EX

www.simonsays.co.uk
www.yuckweb.com

YUCK'S ROTTEN JOKE

"What did you bring?" Yuck asked.

It was Monday morning, and Yuck and Little Eric were sitting at the back of assembly rummaging in their bags.

Little Eric pulled out a small brown packet.

"Itching Powder," Yuck read.

Then Little Eric pulled out a small green packet. "And Sneezing Powder."

5

Yuck took out a Whoopee Cushion, a
bottle of Fake Blood and…

"Check this out," he said. From his bag
Yuck pulled a curling lump of Dogdidapoo.

Little Eric prodded it with his finger. "It looks just like the real thing."

"Watch this."

Yuck reached forward and put the fake dog poo on the floor in front of him, just where Schoolie Julie was about to sit down.

"Watch out, Schoolie Julie!" Yuck said.

Schoolie Julie sat on the Dogdidapoo and jumped back up.

"Schoolie Julie sat in dog poo!" Little Eric giggled.

"What's going on at the back?" Mr Reaper, the headmaster, boomed.

Yuck quickly put the fake dog poo back in his bag.

"Yuck and Eric, come here!" the Reaper told them.

Yuck and Little Eric walked to the front of assembly.

"Hand me your report cards!" the Reaper said.

From his back pocket, Yuck pulled out a folded piece of orange card.

The Reaper snatched it. "That's a star off for messing about in assembly!"

He held Yuck's report card with his fingertips. Its corners were chewed and the cover was smeared in bogies. As the Reaper opened it, his mouth stretched into a grin. "Well, well, you only have one star for good behaviour."

Sure enough, Yuck's report card only had one star stuck in it.

"When did you get a star?" Little Eric whispered.

"I found it on the floor under the Dragon's desk," Yuck whispered back.

The Reaper peeled the star off, then snatched Little Eric's report card.

Little Eric's had two stars stuck in it.

The Reaper peeled one off.

"I've still got one left!" Little Eric whispered to Yuck.

Then the Reaper peeled off Little Eric's last star. "And that's for whispering!"

He held their empty report cards in the air and showed them to the whole school. "At the end of the week I shall be looking at everyone's report cards. Everyone must have at least ten stars or they will be in BIG TROUBLE – they will be punished and a letter will be sent to their parents."

The Reaper handed the report cards back to Yuck and Little Eric.

11

After assembly, Polly Princess and Juicy Lucy ran over to Yuck and Little Eric in the playground. Polly was smiling.

"I've got ten stars!" she said, waving her report card in Yuck's face.

"So have I!" said Lucy.

Inside each of their report cards were ten gold stars.

"So what? I've got this," Yuck said. He pulled a plastic flower from his pocket. "Pretty, isn't it?"

Polly looked at the flower.

Yuck squeezed it and smelly pond water squirted in her face.

Little Eric laughed.

That evening, Polly Princess showed
Mum and Dad her report card. "Yuck's got
no stars and I've got ten. Miss Fortune will
probably give me even more tomorrow."

"That's because you're a goodie-goodie,"
Yuck said. He was sitting at the kitchen
table reading OINK.

Polly stuck her tongue out at Yuck and
stood up to make Mum and Dad a cup
of tea.

Yuck turned the page and giggled.

"Why can't you be helpful like your
sister?" Mum asked.

"I AM helpful," Yuck said. "I'll help Polly with the tea."

He put down his copy of OINK, and from his pocket took out a small plastic packet. On it was written Sugar-Coated Flies. He picked out two lumps and put them in the sugar bowl.

Then he watched as Polly spooned the two sugar lumps into Dad's tea.

"How come you haven't got any stars, Yuck?" Dad asked.

"I have," Yuck said.

Polly handed Mum and Dad their tea. "He's lying."

"Show me your report card, Yuck," Dad told him, taking a sip from his mug.

Yuck rummaged in his pocket. "I must have left it at school."

At that moment, Dad coughed and spat out his tea, spraying it across the room.

"Flies! Polly, there are flies in my tea!" he shouted.

"It wasn't me! It must have been Yuck!"
Polly said.

But Yuck was already running up the
stairs. He threw himself on his bed and
emptied his jokes from his bag.

Yuck decided that when he was
EMPEROR OF EVERYTHING people
would be given stars for playing jokes. He
and Little Eric would have hundreds.
Goodie-goodies would have none. And the
Reaper would be in BIG TROUBLE
because he never played jokes and he was
never ever funny. He'd get no stars at all,
and for his punishment he'd be turned into
a giant dog poo.

At Tuesday breaktime, Yuck and Little Eric sat in a tree at the edge of the playground. They were looking down at a coin that they had glued to the ground.

"Do you really think we can get five stars?" Little Eric asked.

"It's Polly and Lucy who are going to be in BIG TROUBLE," Yuck said.

He had a plan.

Polly Princess and Juicy Lucy were walking to their classroom.

"Ssshhh! They're coming," Little Eric whispered.

Polly spied the coin on the ground and ran over. But when she bent down to pick it up, the coin wouldn't budge.

In the tree, Yuck opened the packet of Sneezing Powder. Little Eric opened the packet of Itching Powder. While Polly struggled with the coin, they sprinkled the powder over her.

"It's stuck," Polly said to Lucy. "ATCHOO!" She was scratching her hair.

"Let me try," Lucy said, bending down to pick up the coin. She dug her nails under it, trying to prise it from the ground.

Yuck and Little Eric sprinkled the powder on her.

"It won't move. ATCHOO!" She was scratching her neck. "We'd better get going or—ATCHOO!—we'll be late for class!"

Polly and Lucy sneezed and scratched across the playground, pushing past everyone as the bell rang for lessons. They were still sneezing and scratching when they ran into class.

"ATCHOO!"

Miss Fortune looked over her glasses at them. "Is something wrong?"

"Nothing, Miss," Polly said, scratching her head. "ATCHOO!"

"We're fine, Miss," Lucy said, scratching her tummy. "ATCHOO!"

"Stop fidgeting," Miss Fortune told them.

But no matter how hard they tried, Polly and Lucy couldn't sit still.

"Is this some kind of joke?" Miss Fortune asked.

"I feel—all—itchy—ATCHOO!" Polly said.

Polly and Lucy stood up and began scratching one another.

"You're behaving like a couple of chimpanzees!" Miss Fortune said. "Stop it this minute!"

But Polly and Lucy couldn't stop sneezing and they couldn't stop scratching.

"Hand me your report cards!" Miss Fortune shouted.

Polly and Lucy took out their report cards and handed them to Miss Fortune.

"I'm surprised at you two."

"ATCHOO!" Polly and Lucy both sneezed over Miss Fortune.

Miss Fortune wiped her face and took a star from each of them.

"But Miss!" Polly moaned. "It's not our fault—ATCHOO!"

At that moment, there was a knock at the classroom door.

It was Yuck and Little Eric.

"Sorry to interrupt, Miss," Yuck said.

"Why aren't you in your lesson?" Miss Fortune asked.

"Because we've come to report a lost coin, Miss."

"We've been guarding it," Little Eric said, "in case of thieves."

"Where is it?"

"In the playground. Polly and Lucy dropped it when they were swinging in the trees."

"We didn't want to pick it up because it isn't ours, Miss," Yuck said.

"That was very good of you," Miss Fortune said. "Polly and Lucy can collect it at lunchbreak. Here, you can have these."

Miss Fortune licked the two stars that she'd taken from Polly and Lucy, and stuck them into Yuck and Little Eric's report cards.

They ran off giggling. "We've got one! We've got one star each! Only nine more to go!"

At lunchtime, Polly and Lucy had to take off their itchy clothes and change into their gym kit. When they went outside to fetch the coin, it had gone. So instead, they decided to play catch.

"I bet it was Yuck," Polly said, throwing the ball.

"I want my star back," Lucy said, catching the ball. "I've only got nine left."

"Yuck's going to be in BIG TROUBLE for this!"

Yuck and Little Eric were alone in Mrs Wagon the Dragon's classroom – she had gone to lunch. They were standing at the window watching Polly and Lucy.

Yuck took a clear strip of sticky tape from his bag. He drew a jagged black line across it, like a crack, and stuck it to the window.

As the Reaper came round the corner on playground patrol, Yuck and Little Eric ran outside.

"Sir, Sir, there's been an accident!" Little Eric called. "I don't know what happened exactly, but we were just doing some extra work in the Dragon's, I mean Mrs Wagon's, room when we heard the sound of breaking glass!"

"What's that, Sir?" Yuck said, looking at the window with the crack stuck across it.

The Reaper pointed. "A broken window!" he boomed. "Mrs Wagon will be furious!"

The Reaper looked over at Polly and Lucy playing catch. "Did you do this?" he asked.

"It wasn't us, Sir!"

"Don't tell fibs. You must have smashed it with your ball. Give me your report cards."

The Reaper took a star each from Polly and Lucy's cards.

"But Sir!" Polly said.

The Reaper turned to Yuck and Little Eric. "You two can have these for being good and doing extra work at lunchtime."

He stuck Polly and Lucy's stars into Yuck and Little Eric's report cards.

"That's not fair!" Lucy said.

Yuck and Little Eric ran off giggling. "We've got two! We've got two stars each! Only eight more to go!"

On Wednesday, Polly and Lucy were tidying the books on Miss Fortune's bookshelf. From the corridor they heard shouting.

"Help!"

"Aarrgghh!"

The girls held each other tightly as the classroom door burst open. It was Yuck and Little Eric. "Help!" they cried. "Help!"

The girls screamed.

Blood was running down Yuck's face. His cheek had a long red scar across it.

Little Eric's ear was hanging off the side of his head.

"Help us!" Yuck cried.

"We've been attacked by a squirrel!" Little Eric added.

"A really big one!" Yuck said, staggering over to Polly and Lucy. "Help! I'm going to faint."

Polly grabbed Yuck's arm to steady him.
The arm came off in her hand.
She screamed.

Little Eric pointed to the door with a
blood-squirting severed finger. "Nurse
Payne! Get Nurse Payne!"

Little Eric closed his eyes and clutched his head.

An eyeball rolled  across the floor.

Polly and Lucy screamed and ran out of the room, down the corridor, all the way to Nurse Payne. "It's Yuck and Little Eric. They've been attacked by a squirrel!"

"By a WHAT?"

"A really big one! Quick! Come quick!"

Nurse Payne grabbed her First-Aid box.

Back in Miss Fortune's classroom, Yuck picked up his Fake Severed Arm and Little Eric picked up his Fake Eyeball. They laughed and wiped the Fake Blood from their faces.

Little Eric put the Fake Severed Ear and the Fake Severed Finger back in his pocket.

They heard footsteps, and pretended to tidy the books on the bookshelf.

"Your scar!" Little Eric said.

Yuck peeled the Fake Scar from his face just as Polly, Lucy and Nurse Payne ran into the room.

"What's going on?" Polly asked. "Where's the blood gone?"

"What are you talking about?" Yuck said. "Little Eric and I were just tidying the shelves for Miss Fortune."

Nurse Payne turned to Polly and Lucy. "I think you two have some explaining to do."

Miss Fortune came in. "What's happening here?" she asked.

"These two girls have been playing tricks," Nurse Payne told her. "They said Yuck and Eric were attacked by a giant squirrel."

"But they were, Miss."

"Ridiculous! Hand me your report cards!" Miss Fortune said. She took a star each from Polly and Lucy's report cards.

"And what are these two doing in here?" she said, looking at Yuck and Little Eric.

"They were just tidying your books for you," Nurse Payne told her.

"What a nice surprise," Miss Fortune said, and she stuck Polly and Lucy's stars into Yuck and Little Eric's report cards. "That was very thoughtful of you."

Yuck and Little Eric laughed and ran off down the corridor.

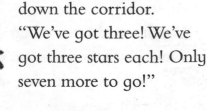

"We've got three! We've got three stars each! Only seven more to go!"

At lunchtime, in the canteen, Polly and Lucy were moaning.

"It's not fair!" Polly said. "They're getting all our stars! I've only got seven left."

Yuck and Little Eric walked over.

"We just wanted to say sorry for what happened earlier," Yuck said.

"It was only meant to be a joke," Little Eric said.

"Then give our stars back," Lucy told them.

"How about we give you these instead, to say sorry?"

Yuck handed Lucy a bag of sweets.

"Don't think you can get away with it that easily," Lucy told him, snatching the bag from Yuck.

"We know what you're up to," Polly said, unwrapping a sweet and chewing it. "And when the Reaper finds out he'll take away ALL your stars and you'll be in BIG TROUBLE."

Yuck and Little Eric went and sat down.

"I didn't know you had sweets," Little Eric said.

"Not ordinary sweets – Extra-hot Sweets!" Yuck said.

By the time Polly and Lucy had got their lunch and sat down at their table, they'd both eaten three sweets each.

"Do you feel a bit hot?" Polly asked. "My mouth's burning."

"I feel… ON FIRE!" Lucy replied. Sweat was pouring down her face.

From his bag Little Eric took out what looked like a lumpy plastic puddle. "Fake Sick. Watch this."

Little Eric sneaked the Fake Sick onto the table next to Polly.

Her face was bright purple. "I feel ill," she said.

"Me too," Lucy said, and she pointed. "Is that what I think it is?"

"It looks like—BLURGH!"

Polly was sick in her hands.

Lucy was sick on Polly.

Mrs Dollop the dinner-lady ran over.
"What have you been eating?" she asked.

Polly couldn't speak. She threw the bag
of sweets on the table.

Little Eric glanced at Yuck and gave him a thumbs-up.

Yuck ran out to the playground to find the Reaper. "Polly and Lucy have been sick, Sir," he said.

Meanwhile, Little Eric picked up the Fake Sick, wiped it clean and put it back in his bag.

The Reaper came running in. He looked at the sick all over the table and then at the bag of sweets. "Polly and Lucy! That's a star off for each of you, for eating sweets before lunch!"

"But Sir…" Polly gasped.

The Reaper took a star from Polly and Lucy's report cards. "Now, go and clean yourselves up, you greedy girls."

Yuck picked up the bag of Extra-hot Sweets from the table, holding his hand over the label. "Do you want Polly's sweets, Sir?"

"I expect you'll want to confiscate them," Little Eric said.

"Good idea," the Reaper said.

He took the bag of sweets and gave Yuck and Little Eric a star each for being helpful. Then he went back outside to patrol the playground.

Yuck and Little Eric watched from the window, giggling as the Reaper unwrapped a sweet and popped it into his mouth.

"We've got four! We've got four stars each! Only six more to go!"

On Thursday, Yuck and Little Eric arrived early at school.

They were first to assembly. As Polly sat down, Yuck slipped a Whoopee Cushion underneath her bottom.

RRRRRRRRIP! It let off a loud raspberry.

Polly jumped up and Yuck cracked a Stink Bomb.

"What's going on over there?" the Reaper boomed.

"Polly farted, Sir," Yuck said.

"It smells, Sir!" Little Eric said.

Lucy pulled the Whoopee Cushion from underneath Polly and held it up.

"It was this, Sir," she said.

"You know it's forbidden to play practical jokes in school!"

"But it's not mine, Sir!" Lucy said.

Yuck slipped the packet of Stink Bombs into Polly's bag.

The Reaper ran over, holding his nose.

"Haven't you two caused enough trouble this week?" he said to Polly and Lucy.

"But it wasn't us!"

"Empty your bags!"

Polly and Lucy turned their bags upside down.

"See, Sir, just books and a hairbrush and our pencil cases and—"

"Stink Bombs!" the Reaper boomed. "Right, that's another star off for each of you."

"But it's him, Sir — it's all Yuck's fault," Polly protested.

Yuck and Little Eric stood up. "Can we have a star please, Sir?"

"What for?"

"For opening all the windows, Sir," Yuck said. "It stinks in here!"

"That's very thoughtful of you. Here, you can have one star each."

Assembly was evacuated while the stink cleared.

"We've got five! We've got five stars each!" Yuck and Little Eric ran around the playground.

"I've never had five stars before!" Little Eric said.

"Soon we'll have ten stars each," Yuck said.

42

"How?" Little Eric asked.

"We'll play a big joke – a big ROTTEN JOKE!" Yuck said.

He whispered something into Little Eric's ear, and Little Eric giggled.

For the rest of the day Polly and Lucy stayed in Miss Fortune's classroom.

"It's not fair. Yuck and Little Eric have got as many stars as us now!" Lucy said.

Polly whispered in Lucy's ear: "I know how we can get them back…"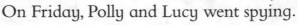

On Friday, Polly and Lucy went spying.

"We'll catch them red-handed," Polly said. "When the Reaper finds out what they've been up to, Yuck and Little Eric will be in BIG TROUBLE."

In assembly, they saw Yuck and Little Eric giggling.

"They're planning another joke," Polly said.

43

During breaktime, Polly and Lucy saw Yuck and Little Eric go to Mr Sweep's store cupboard and fetch a bucket.

"What do you think they're doing with Sweepy's bucket?" Lucy asked.

At lunchtime Polly and Lucy followed
Yuck and Little Eric round the back of the
kitchens and watched as they filled the
bucket with
the week's
leftovers:
custard and
baked beans,
yoghurt and
chips, lumpy
gravy, cheesy
pizza – and
ROTTEN EGGS!

"Now we need to hide it," Polly and
Lucy heard Yuck say. "Until after lunch."

"Where?" Little Eric asked.

"The Reaper's office!" Yuck said.

"Are you crazy?"

"The Reaper's on playground patrol all
lunchtime. It's the last place anyone will
look. We'll fetch it when the bell goes and
gunk Polly and Lucy on their way into
class."

Polly and Lucy looked at one another.
"We've got them!" Lucy said.

They followed Yuck and Little Eric to the
Reaper's office, then hid behind a large
plant in the corridor and watched as Yuck
nudged the door open.

"It's all clear," he said.

Yuck and Little Eric crept inside and closed the door behind them.

"Did they follow us?" Little Eric whispered.

"They've been following us all morning," Yuck whispered back.

Polly and Lucy tiptoed out from behind the plant, pressed their ears to the door and listened.

Inside, in a loud voice, Yuck was speaking: "Let's hide the bucket under the desk. When the bell goes we'll collect it, and then gunk Polly and Lucy on their way into class."

"But how are we going to gunk them without being seen?" Little Eric asked loudly.

"We'll balance the bucket on top of their classroom door. Polly and Lucy are always first to class. They'll get covered."

Polly and Lucy looked at one another.

The door handle turned.

"Quick, hide!" Polly whispered.

Polly and Lucy hid behind the plant as Yuck and Little Eric came out of the Reaper's office and wandered off down the corridor.

Polly and Lucy sneaked inside.

They looked under the Reaper's desk.

"There's the bucket," Lucy said. "Let's tell on them."

"We'll do better than that," Polly said.

She pointed at the door. "You heard what they said. They'll be coming back later. Quick – get the bucket!"

Polly stood on a chair next to the door and Lucy handed the bucket up to her.

"When they come back to fetch it, they'll get gunked!" Polly said.

She opened the door just a little bit and stretched as high as she could, balancing the bucket on top of the door.

"Perfect!" Lucy said.

"And when the Reaper sees them, he'll tell them off for messing about in his office. They'll be in BIG TROUBLE!"

"And we'll get stars for catching them," Lucy said.

Polly and Lucy hid under the Reaper's desk and waited.

"Sshhh!" Polly said. "I can hear them coming."

Yuck and Little Eric were walking back along the corridor.

"What are they doing with a bucket in my office?" the Reaper was asking.

"I don't know. But they looked like they were up to no good," Yuck said.

The door to the Reaper's office was slightly open.

The Reaper took a step forward and pushed on the handle.

Yuck and Little Eric took a step back.

As the door swung open, the bucket fell on the Reaper's head with a SPLASH!

Gunk poured all over him. Custard, gravy and baked beans splattered his bald head. Pizza, yoghurt and chips slid down his face. He stank of rotten eggs!

The Reaper wiped his eyes and saw Polly and Lucy hiding under his desk.

"Is this meant to be a joke?" he asked.

Polly Princess and Juicy Lucy jumped up.

"GIVE ME YOUR REPORT CARDS!"

"But, Sir, it wasn't us!" they told him.

The Reaper snatched their report cards and peeled off ALL their stars.

"Polly and Lucy, you are in BIG TROUBLE!" he said. "I shall be writing to your parents immediately!"

"Do we get a reward, Sir?" Yuck asked. "For helping you catch them."

The Reaper stuck Lucy's stars in Little Eric's report card and Polly's stars in Yuck's.

"We've got ten!" Yuck said. "We've got ten stars each!"

Win Yuck's competition!

KNOW ANY ROTTEN JOKES?

Want to win a complete set of Yuck books,
signed by authors Matt and Dave,
plus a special Yuck goody bag full to the brim
with jokes, yucky goodies and gross gadgets?

Then log on to the Yuck website and enter
Yuck's Rotten Joke Competition!

Tell us your most rotten joke ever and you
could be a winner!

 Here's one of Yuck's favourites:

Q. Why is football such a yucky sport?

A. Because you dribble a lot!

Visit www.yuckweb.com

Be warned: it's really Yucky!

Become a member of Yuck's fanclub at:
WWW.YUCKWEB.COM
Find Matt and Dave's rotten jokes, gross games and disgusting downloads, as well as crazy competitions AND the first word on Yuck's new adventures.

Now Yuck has a trick up his sleeve for you. . .

Hold this book in one hand.

Pick your nose.

Close the book and **flip it over**

Shout **ROCKITS** and it becomes another book!

Before she goes, Winnie would like to teach you one of her favourite spells—turning one book into another!

First of all, make sure you're holding this book.

Stamp your foot,
shout 'Abracadabra'.
Now for the tricky bit!
Close the book and
flip it over.
Good luck — hope it
works for you!

Get a guided
tour of
Winnie's
house . . .

and browse
the pictures
in her gallery.

Find out about
all of Winnie's
books . . .

or click on
'Fun Stuff' for
jokes, games, and
much more.